I KNOW A WEE PIGGY

COUNTY FAIR

→ WELCOME →

by Kim Norman   pictures by Henry Cole

Dial Books for Young Readers   an imprint of Penguin Group (USA) Inc.

For my dear Doris and Atwill,
and our beautiful Smithfield –K.N.

For Massimo Cesare Chirighin
...augurandovi molte avventure felici! –H.C.

DIAL BOOKS FOR YOUNG READERS

A division of Penguin Young Readers Group · Published by The Penguin Group

Penguin Group (USA) Inc., 375 Hudson Street, New York, NY 10014, U.S.A.

Penguin Group (Canada), 90 Eglinton Avenue East, Suite 700, Toronto, Ontario, Canada M4P 2Y3 (a division of Pearson Penguin Canada Inc.)

Penguin Books Ltd, 80 Strand, London WC2R 0RL, England

Penguin Ireland, 25 St. Stephen's Green, Dublin 2, Ireland (a division of Penguin Books Ltd)

Penguin Group (Australia), 250 Camberwell Road, Camberwell, Victoria 3124, Australia (a division of Pearson Australia Group Pty Ltd)

Penguin Books India Pvt Ltd, 11 Community Centre, Panchsheel Park, New Delhi - 110 017, India

Penguin Group (NZ), 67 Apollo Drive, Rosedale, Auckland 0632, New Zealand (a division of Pearson New Zealand Ltd)

Penguin Books (South Africa) (Pty) Ltd, 24 Sturdee Avenue, Rosebank, Johannesburg 2196, South Africa

Penguin Books Ltd, Registered Offices: 80 Strand, London WC2R 0RL, England

Text copyright © 2012 by Kim Norman

Pictures copyright © 2012 by Henry Cole

Text set in Coop Light

Manufactured in China on acid-free paper

3 5 7 9 10 8 6 4 2

Library of Congress Cataloging-in-Publication Data

Norman, Kimberly.

I know a wee piggy / by Kim Norman ; pictures by Henry Cole.

p. cm.

Summary: A cumulative, rhyming tale of an ordinary pig who leaps out of his boy's arms at a state fair and wallows in color after color, turning himself into a work of art.

ISBN 978-0-8037-3735-8 (hardcover)

Special Markets ISBN 978-0-8037-4040-2 Not For Resale

[1. Stories in rhyme. 2. Pigs–Fiction. 3. Agricultural exhibitions–Fiction. 4. Colors.] I. Cole, Henry, 1955- ill. II. Title.

PZ8.3.N7498Iak 2014

[E]–dc23   2011029977

The artwork was created in acrylic paints and colored pencil on Arches hot press watercolor paper.

This Imagination Library edition is published by Penguin Group (USA), a Pearson company, exclusively for Dolly Parton's Imagination Library, a not-for-profit program designed to inspire a love of reading and learning, sponsored in part by The Dollywood Foundation. Penguin's trade editions of this work are available wherever books are sold.

I know a wee piggy . . .

who wallowed in **BROWN**.

Upside down, he wallowed in **brown**.

"But **brown** is not for me," he said. "I think I'll add a rinse of . . ."

RED!

I know a wee piggy who wallowed in **red**.
Hoof to head, he wallowed in **red**.

He wallowed in **red** to go with the **brown**.
Upside down, he wallowed in **brown**.

Piggy said, "The **red**'s too bright. I think I'll add a wash of . . ."

WHITE!

I know a wee piggy who wallowed in white.
It's not polite to wallow in white.

He wallowed in white to go with the **red**.
He wallowed in **red** to go with the **brown**.
Upside down, he wallowed in **brown**.

Piggy said, "Too pale, I think. I'd better add a pinch of . . ."

PINK!

I know a wee piggy who wallowed in pink.
How silly to think he needed more pink.

He wallowed in pink to go with the white.
He wallowed in white to go with the red.
He wallowed in red to go with the brown.
Upside down, he wallowed in brown.

"Pink's a bore!" I heard him bellow. "I need about a yard of . . ."

YELLOW!

I know a wee piggy who wallowed in yellow.
Slippery fellow, to wallow in yellow.

He wallowed in yellow to go with the pink.
He wallowed in pink to go with the white.
He wallowed in white to go with the red.
He wallowed in red to go with the brown.
Upside down, he wallowed in brown.

Piggy squealed, "I won't look back until I add a blast of . . ."

BLACK!

I know a wee piggy who wallowed in **black**.
Out by a shack, he wallowed in **black**.

He wallowed in **black** to go with the yellow.
He wallowed in yellow to go with the pink.
He wallowed in pink to go with the white.
He wallowed in white to go with the red.
He wallowed in red to go with the brown.
Upside down, he wallowed in **brown**.

Piggy shouted, "Now I've seen that I should add a glimpse of . . ."

GREEN!

I know a wee piggy who wallowed in **green**.
Oh, what a scene! He'll NEVER get clean!

He wallowed in **green** to go with the **black**.
He wallowed in **black** to go with the yellow.
He wallowed in yellow to go with the pink.
He wallowed in pink to go with the white.
He wallowed in white to go with the **red**.
He wallowed in **red** to go with the **brown**.
Upside down, he wallowed in **brown**.

Piggy sighed. "The **green's** okay, but now I need a glob of . . ."

GRAY!

I know a wee piggy who wallowed in **gray**.
Orange and **gray**, a brilliant display.

UH-OH . . .

GET OUT
OF HIS WAY!

I know a wee piggy who didn't stop there. . . .

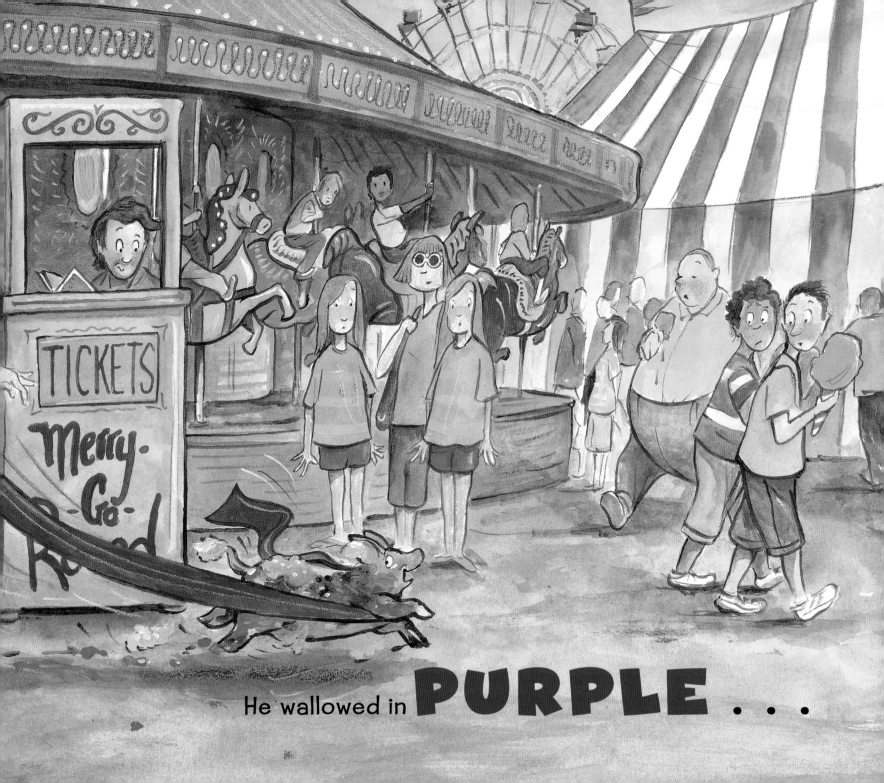

He wallowed in **PURPLE** . . .

ALL OVER THE FAIR!

He added the **purple** . . .

. . . to go with the gray.

He added the gray . . .

. . . to go with the green.

He added the green . . .

. . . to go with the **black**.

He added the **black** . . .

. . . to go with the yellow.

He added the yellow . .

. . . to go with the pink.

He added the pink . . .

. . . to go with the white.

He added the white . . .

. . . to go with the red.

He added the red . . .

. . . to go with the brown.

Upside down, he wallowed in **brown.**

Piggy said, "I'm not quite through. I won't be till I add some . . ."

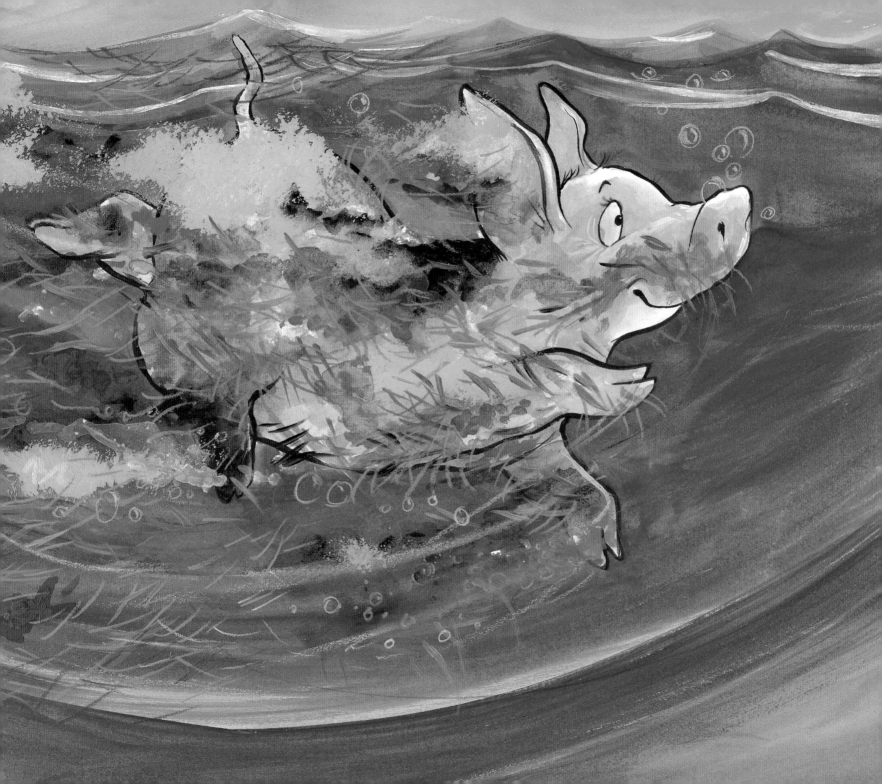

BLUE!

I know a wee piggy who wallowed in **blue**. . . .

He won it, too!